CITY KITTY CAT

To the City

For Emily, with love
—S. W.

For Clara and Fanette
—M. L. H.

SIMON & SCHUSTER BOOKS FOR YOUNG READERS
An imprint of Simon & Schuster Children's Publishing Division
1230 Avenue of the Americas, New York, New York 10020
Text copyright © 2014 by Steve Webb
Illustrations copyright © 2014 by Magali Le Huche
Originally published as *Happy Zappa Cat* in 2014 in Great Britain
by Simon & Schuster UK Ltd.
First US edition 2015
SIMON & SCHUSTER BOOKS FOR YOUNG READERS is a trademark of Simon & Schuster, Inc.
For information about special discounts for bulk purchases, please contact Simon & Schuster
Special Sales at 1-866-506-1949 or business@simonandschuster.com.
The Simon & Schuster Speakers Bureau can bring authors to your live event. For more
information or to book an event, contact the Simon & Schuster Speakers Bureau at
1-866-248-3049 or visit our website at www.simonspeakers.com.
The text for this book is set in Grandma.
Manufactured in China / 0315 SCP
10 9 8 7 6 5 4 3 2 1
Library of Congress Cataloging-in-Publication Data
Webb, Steve, 1967-
City Kitty Cat / Steve Webb ; illustrated by Magali Le Huche.
pages cm
"A Paula Wiseman Book."
Summary: "City Kitty Cat has always loved living and driving his cab in the city.
But when some new friends convince him to visit their jungle home, will Kitty
be able to adjust?"— Provided by publisher.
ISBN 978-1-4814-4331-9 (hardcover) — ISBN 978-1-4814-4332-6 (e-book)
[1. Stories in rhyme. 2. Cats—Fiction. 3. City and town life—Fiction. 4. Voyages and
travels—Fiction. 5. Jungles—Fiction.] I. Le Huche, Magali, 1979- illustrator. II. Title.
PZ7.1.W42Cit 2015   [E]—dc23   2014032405

CITY
KITTY
CAT

STEVE WEBB

Illustrated by

MAGALI LE HUCHE

A PAULA WISEMAN BOOK
SIMON & SCHUSTER BOOKS FOR YOUNG READERS
New York   London   Toronto   Sydney   New Delhi

City kitty, city kitty, city kitty cat,
zipping through the city in his city kitty cab.

"I am the city kitty," sang the happy city cat.
"A zippy city kitty cat, my city cab is pretty fab.
City kitty, city kitty, city kitty cat!"

MARKET

"I zip all over town, then back to the taxi sign.
Each time that I return, new faces wait in line.

"Today there are some giraffes,
some jumbos, and a gator.
I wonder where they'll want to go?
Taxi line, see you later!"

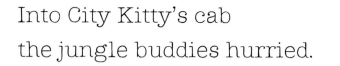

Into City Kitty's cab
the jungle buddies hurried.

He noticed in his mirror
that they looked a little worried.

"Don't you like the city?" he asked, and turned his head.
The passengers all sighed, and this is what they said . . .

"We came to ride a train,
to walk the streets and see the sights.
We came to catch a show
and watch the pretty city lights!

"We've seen the shops, the museum,
and the gallery of art.

We've been to Café Posh Nosh,
for their famous cherry tart!"

"Then, whatever is the matter?"
City Kitty said, and smiled.

All the passengers together cried,
"We really miss the wild!
Please hurry to the airport;
we have to get away.

Our home is where our friends are.
We have to leave today."

Zipping through the city, on their way to catch a plane,
the animals began to smile, heading home again.

"I've never left the city," said Kitty thoughtfully.
"Maybe there's another world I really need to see?"

"Hop aboard this plane with us,"
   his new friends said, and smiled.
"Come for an adventure,
   come and try the wild!"

City Kitty left his cab and the city far behind,
and flew across the world to see what he would find.

Over oceans, over mountains, over trees and waterfalls,
Kitty stared from the window at the wonder of it all.

They landed in the jungle
on a runway made of mud,
with a rattle and a bump
and with not a little thud.

They grabbed a jungle taxi and weaved throughout the trees.
A wild gorilla ride and a rather tight squeeze!

They danced through the jungle
and across a sunny plain.
They splashed through a swamp at night,
then did it all again!

There were stories at the campfire
when the day was done,

great big hairy spider friends,
and swimming gators in the sun.

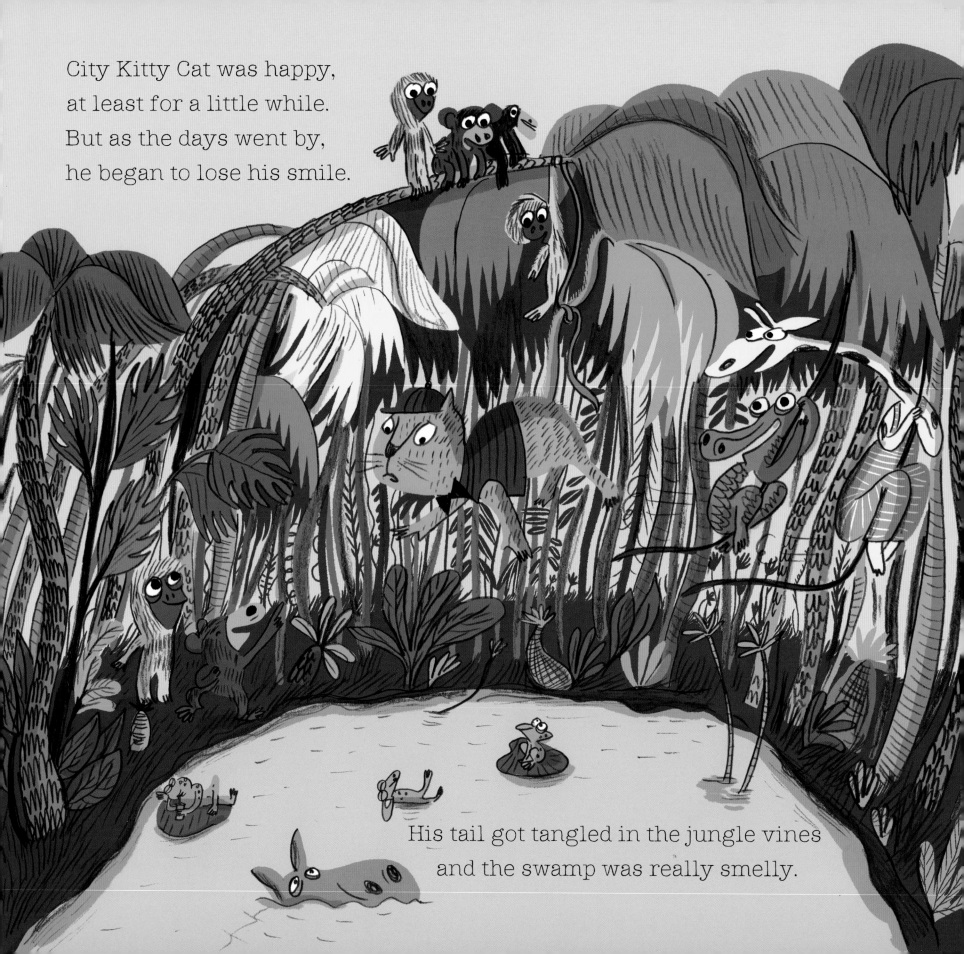

City Kitty Cat was happy,
at least for a little while.
But as the days went by,
he began to lose his smile.

His tail got tangled in the jungle vines
and the swamp was really smelly.

The sunny plains were way too hot;
he had an aching belly.

All the others felt so happy back in their jungle home,
leaving only City Kitty sitting sadly all alone.

"What's the matter, City Kitty?"
asked the monkeys from the trees.
"Whatever is the matter? Won't you tell us, please?"

"I'll tell you what's the matter," City Kitty sobbed, and said,
"I miss the pretty city lights, I miss my comfy bed.

"I miss the shops, the museum,
and the gallery of art.
I miss Café Posh Nosh
and their famous cherry tart!

The wild is pretty perfect
for an adventure holiday,
but the city is the place for me.
I have to get away."

So the giraffes and the zebras and the jumbos and the gator took Kitty to the airport and said, "We'll see you later."

"I'll send a postcard from the city. I'll miss you all so much."
City Kitty waved good-bye and said he'd keep in touch.

A little later, from the window,
City Kitty's cab came into view.
It was parked right where he'd left it,
looking bright and new.

"I am the city kitty," sang the happy city cat.
"Zipping through the city in my city kitty cab.

"No matter where I wander, no matter where I roam,
I am the city kitty cat . . .

...there's no place like home."